MEG goes to BED

for Alexander

MEG goes to BED

by Helen Nicoll
and Jan Pieńkowski

PUFFIN BOOKS

This is where they live

This is what she put in

a nettle

a dandelion

flour

tomatoes

The
supper
wriggled
away

Meg got into bed and went to sleep

Mog and Owl were hungry

Cuckoo

ZZZ

tip
toe
tip
toe
tip
toe

Mog and Owl crept out

POUNCE

Mog tried to catch a mouse

So did Owl

SWOOOP

Mog and Owl tried again

They made pancakes

and then they tossed them

Goodbye!